Adapted by Laura Driscoll
Based on the teleplay
Dolphin Talk by Dennis Garvey
and Tommy Nichols
Illustrated by
Alisa Klayman-Grodsky

Based on the
"Stanley" books
created by Griff
with ticktock Publishing, Ltd.

For information address Disney Press,
114 Fifth Avenue, New York, New York 10011-5690.

Printed in the United States of America

First Edition

1 2 3 4 5 6 7 8 9 10

Library of Congress Catalog Card Number: 2002101320

ISBN: 0-7868-4504-X

Stanley was wild about animals. He knew everything there was to know about lions, kangaroos, camels, and every other creature on earth.

But Stanley especially loved his own pets: his dog, Harry; his goldfish, Dennis; and his cat, Elsie.

So, when Harry's birthday arrived, Stanley said, "We should give him a surprise party!" Stanley, Dennis, and Elsie, along with their friends, Marci and Mimi, started to plan it right away.

The only problem was, Harry kept walking by while they were planning it.

"Hey, dudes. What's happening?" Harry would say. Then everyone would freeze and stop talking.

The first time it happened, Harry just shrugged and went to get a snack.

The second time it happened, Harry gave them a strange look.

The third time, Harry said, “Hmm . . . ,” and rubbed his chin.

How were they going to make plans without his finding out? Stanley, Dennis, and Elsie discussed the problem up in Stanley's room.

"What we need," said Dennis, "is a way of talking to one another, so Harry won't hear what we're saying."

“That’s it!” Stanley exclaimed. “Dolphins talk to each other without words all the time!”

Just then, Marci and Mimi came in . . . with Harry right behind them.

Stanley said, “We were just going to look up how dolphins communicate without using words.” Marci and Mimi understood the plan right away.

So, Stanley got out his favorite book, *The Great Big Book of Everything*. "*A . . . B . . . C . . .*" he said, as he turned the pages of the book, ". . . *D*—Dolphins! Here they are!"

Then, while Elsie and Harry stayed behind, Stanley, Dennis, Marci, and Mimi leaped into the book . . .

. . . and each of them landed on the back of a bottle-nosed dolphin!

As they rode along, Dennis told them all about dolphins. They learned that dolphins are powerful swimmers. . . .

Dolphins live in family groups called pods. . . .

And dolphins can communicate with one another by making squealing, buzzing, clicking, and grunting sounds.

When the dolphins dove underwater, Stanley, Dennis, Mimi, and Marci could hear them making clicking sounds.

“They’re using something called ‘echolocation,’” said Dennis. “The sounds bounce off an object and let the dolphin know where the object is.”

Finally, they saw that dolphins could be taught to understand hand signals made by humans.

"Hey!" Stanley exclaimed. "That's what we need—hand signals!"

At that, they all jumped back into . . .

. . . Stanley's bedroom.

"When I give the thumbs-up sign, that means the coast is clear," Stanley said to Marci and Mimi.

Later that afternoon, as Harry napped in the backyard, Stanley flashed the thumbs-up signal to Marci and Mimi next door.

"We can bring the cake over to Stanley's," Mimi said to Marci.

Ever so quietly, they carried the birthday cake and some balloons across Stanley's backyard and through the back door. When Harry woke up, he ran into the house to find . . .

"SURPRISE!" everyone shouted.

"Happy birthday, Harry!" said Stanley.

"Are you surprised?" Elsie asked Harry.

Harry scratched his head. "I sure am," he said. "I didn't even remember it was my birthday!"

They all had such a great time at Harry's party that Stanley, Dennis, and Elsie were still talking about it at bedtime that night.

"He really *was* surprised, wasn't he?" said Dennis, motioning to Harry who was asleep in Stanley's bed.

"Didn't suspect a thing," Elsie replied.

“Good thing we learned about dolphins today,” said Stanley.

Then Stanley settled down into bed and said good night to his three favorite animals.

Dennis smiled. “And good night to you, Dolphin Boy Stanley!” he said.

DID YOU KNOW?

- Dolphins do not chew their food. They swallow it whole.
- A dolphin breathes through a hole on top of its head called a *blowhole*.
- Dolphins have very small ears, which are located behind their eyes.
- A dolphin is able to jump as high as twenty feet in the air.

FILL IN THE PUZZLE WITH THE WORDS BELOW:

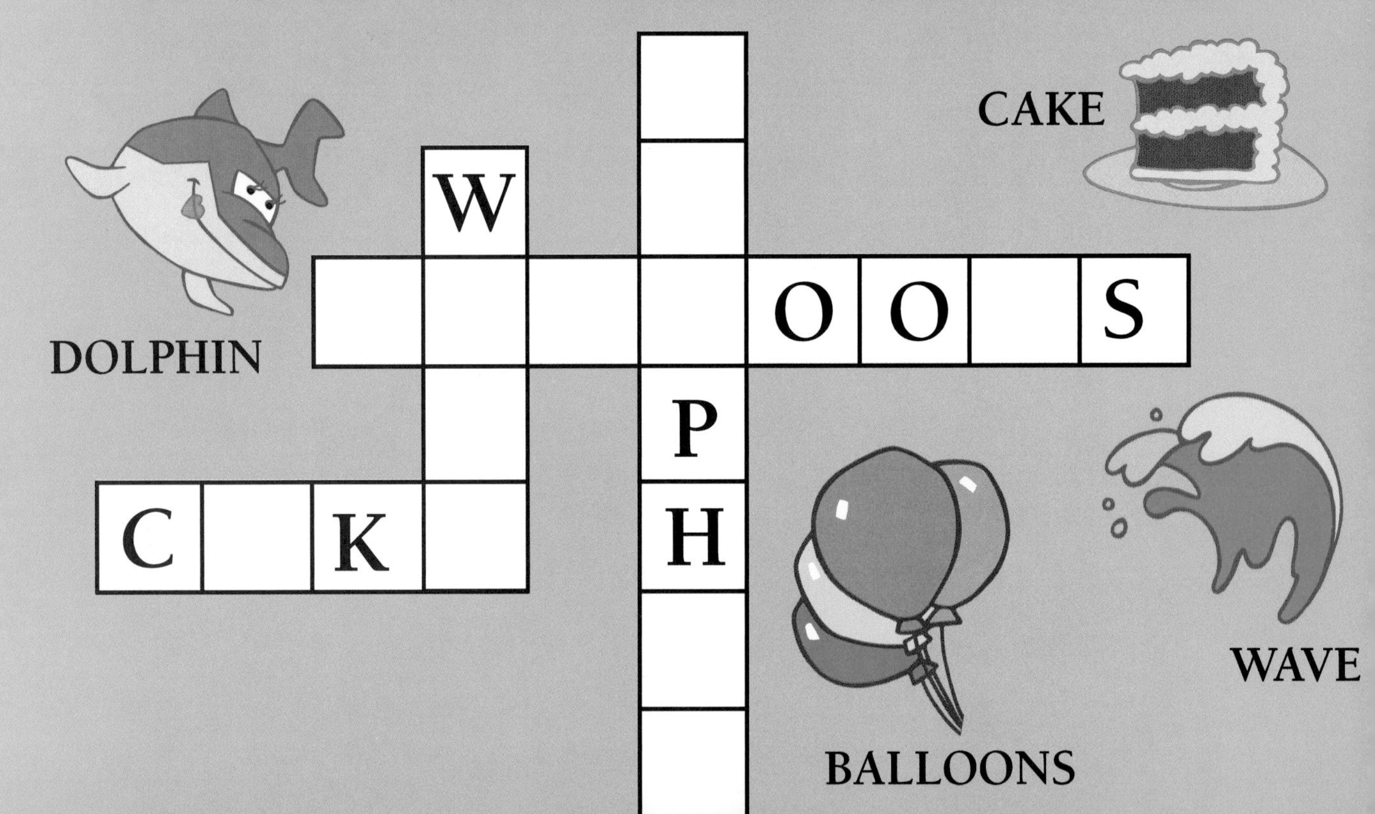